TWO DUMB DUCKS

by

MAXWELL EATON III

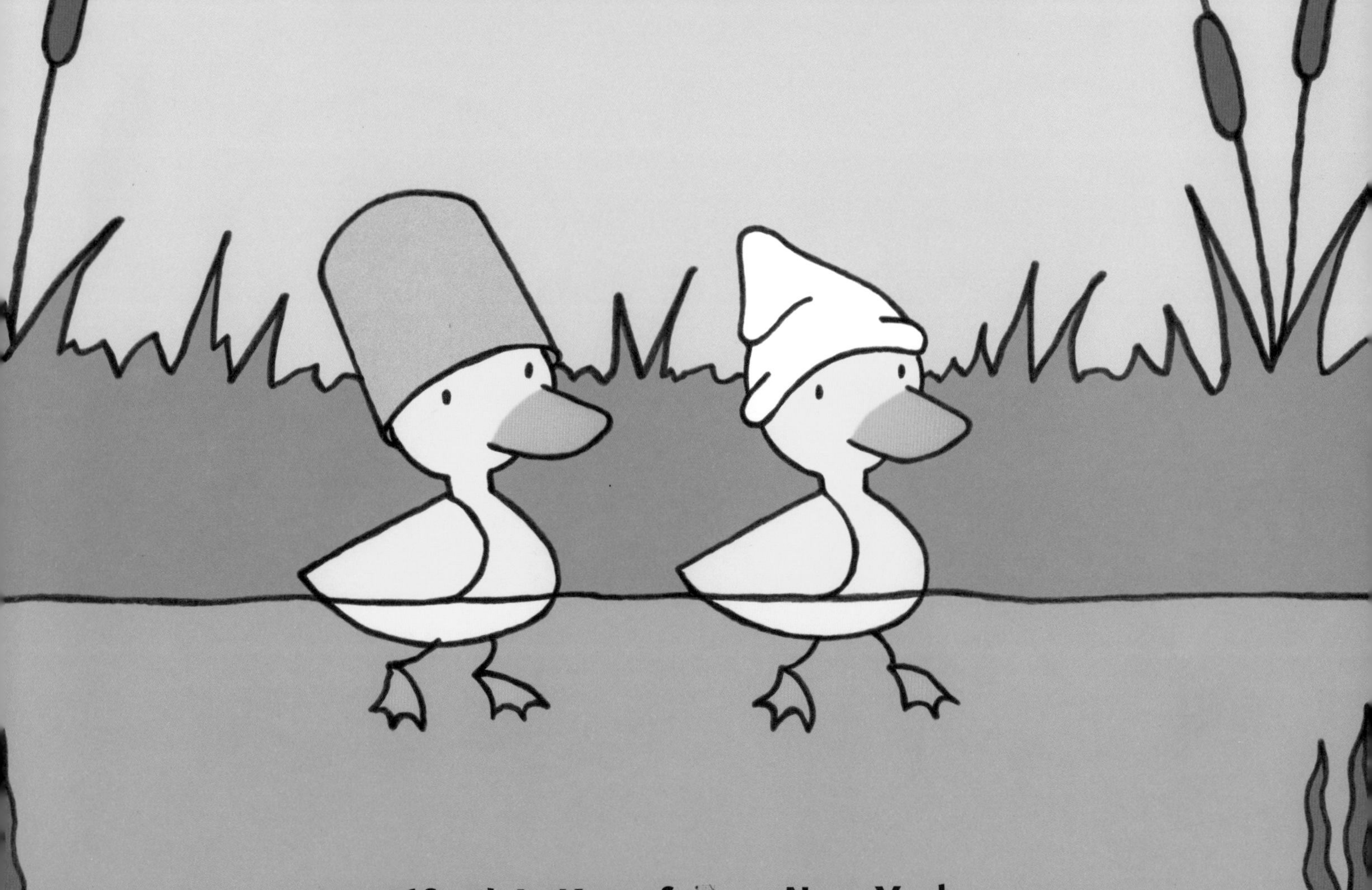

Alfred A. Knopf New York

Steve and Carl are ducks.

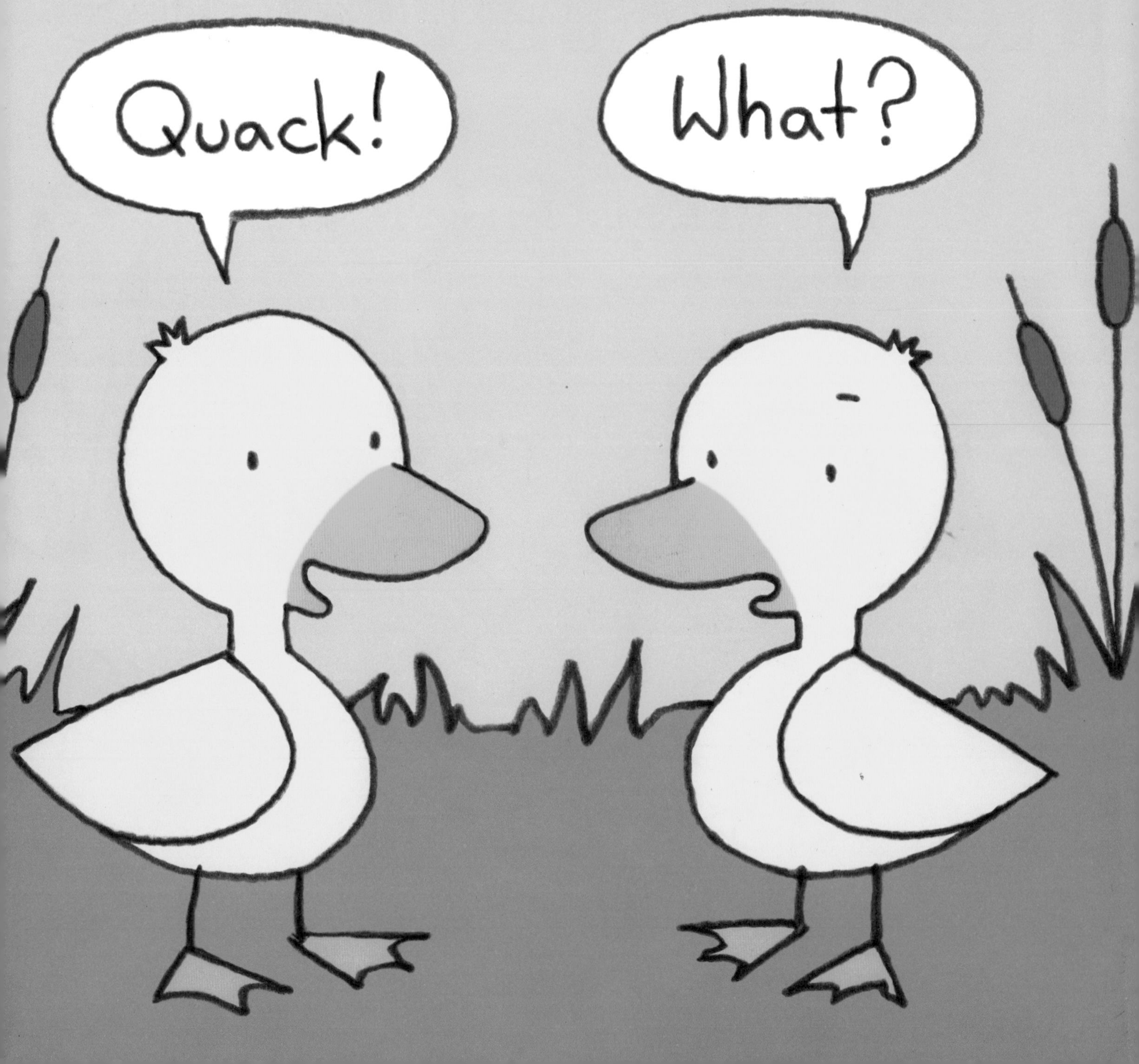
Quack!
What?

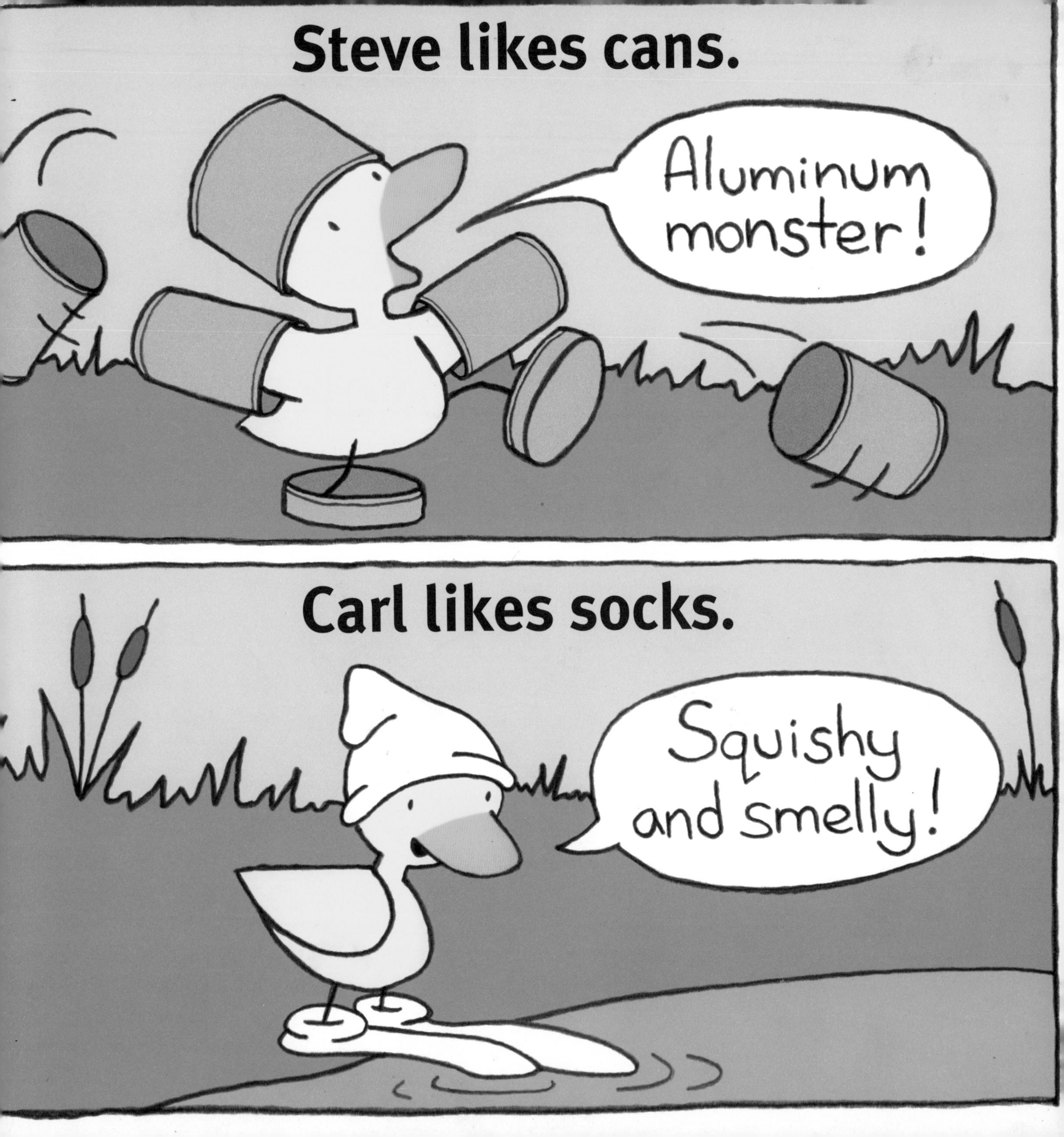
Steve likes cans.
Aluminum monster!
Carl likes socks.
Squishy and smelly!

**They do not like seagulls.
Seagulls call them . . .**

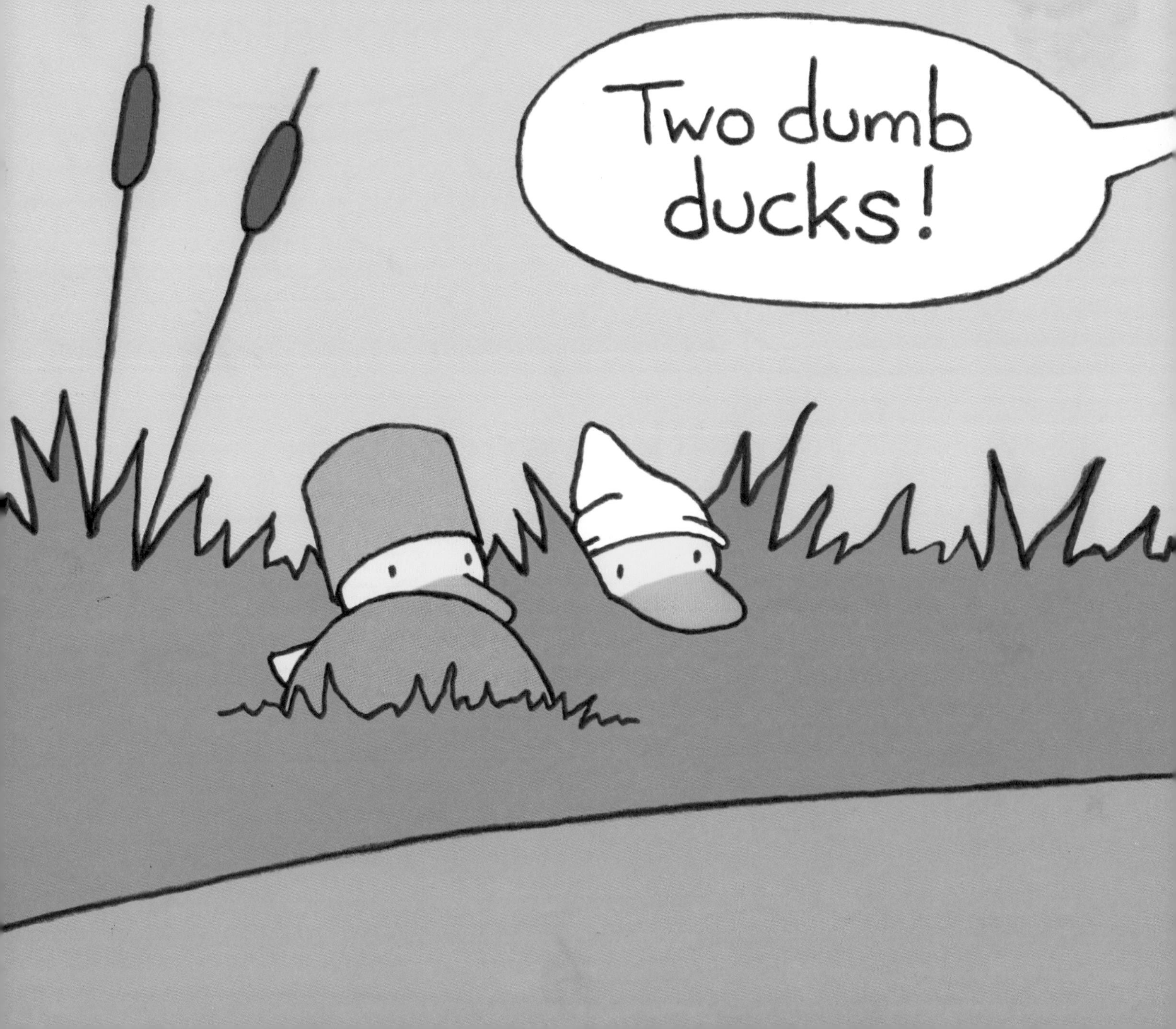
Two dumb ducks!

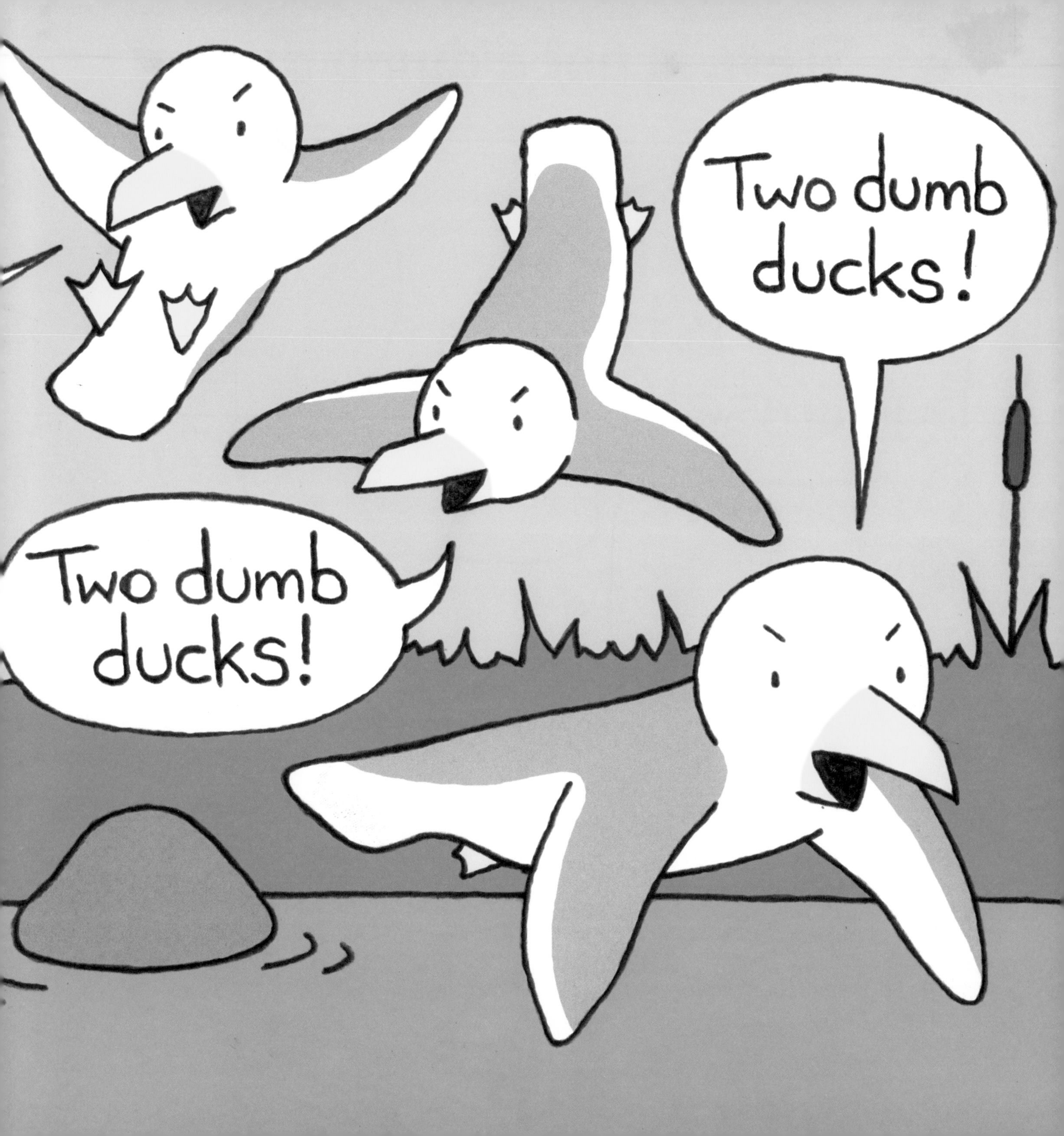
Two dumb ducks!
Two dumb ducks!

Steve is not a dumb duck.

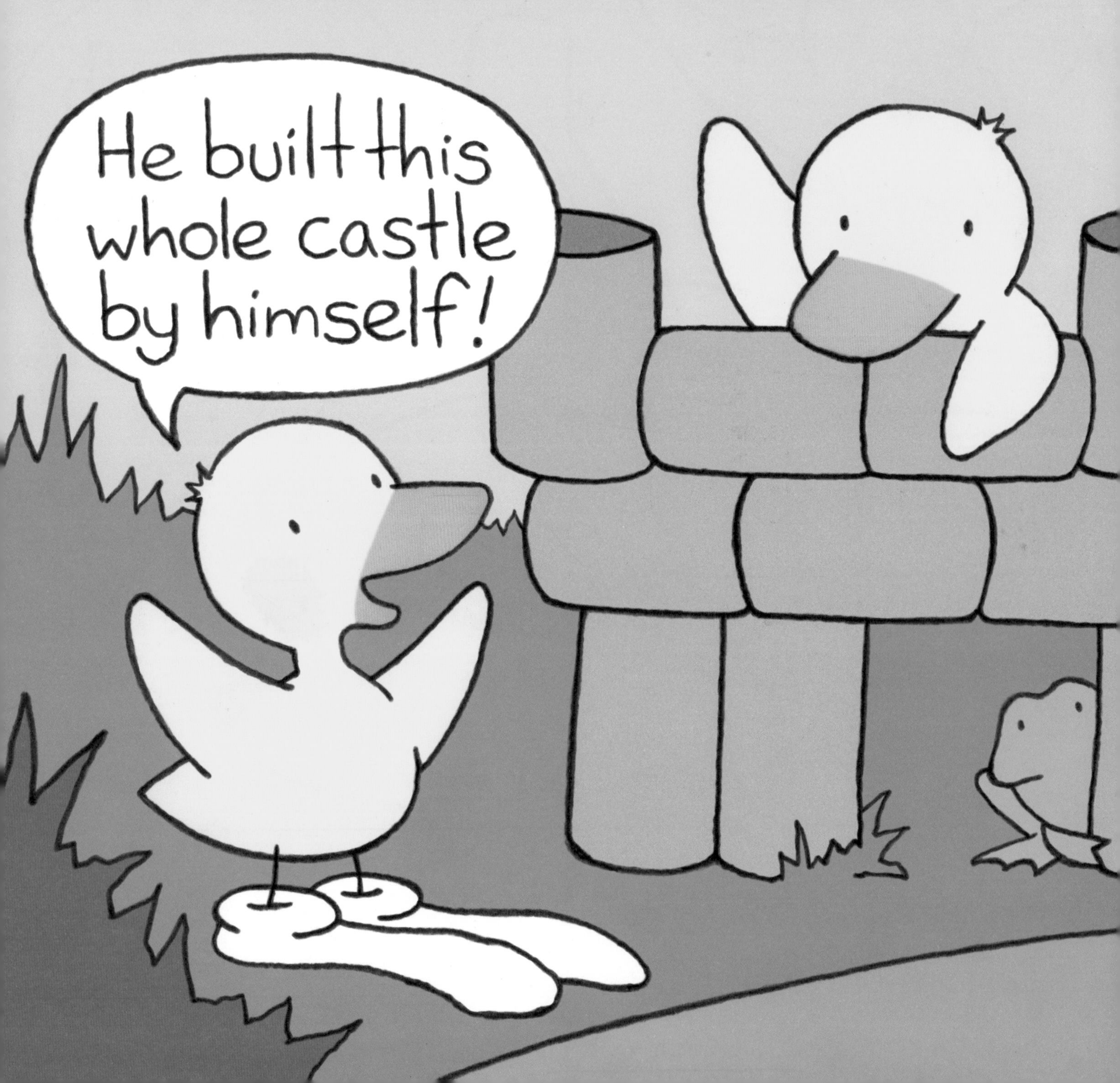
He built this whole castle by himself!

Carl is not a dumb duck.

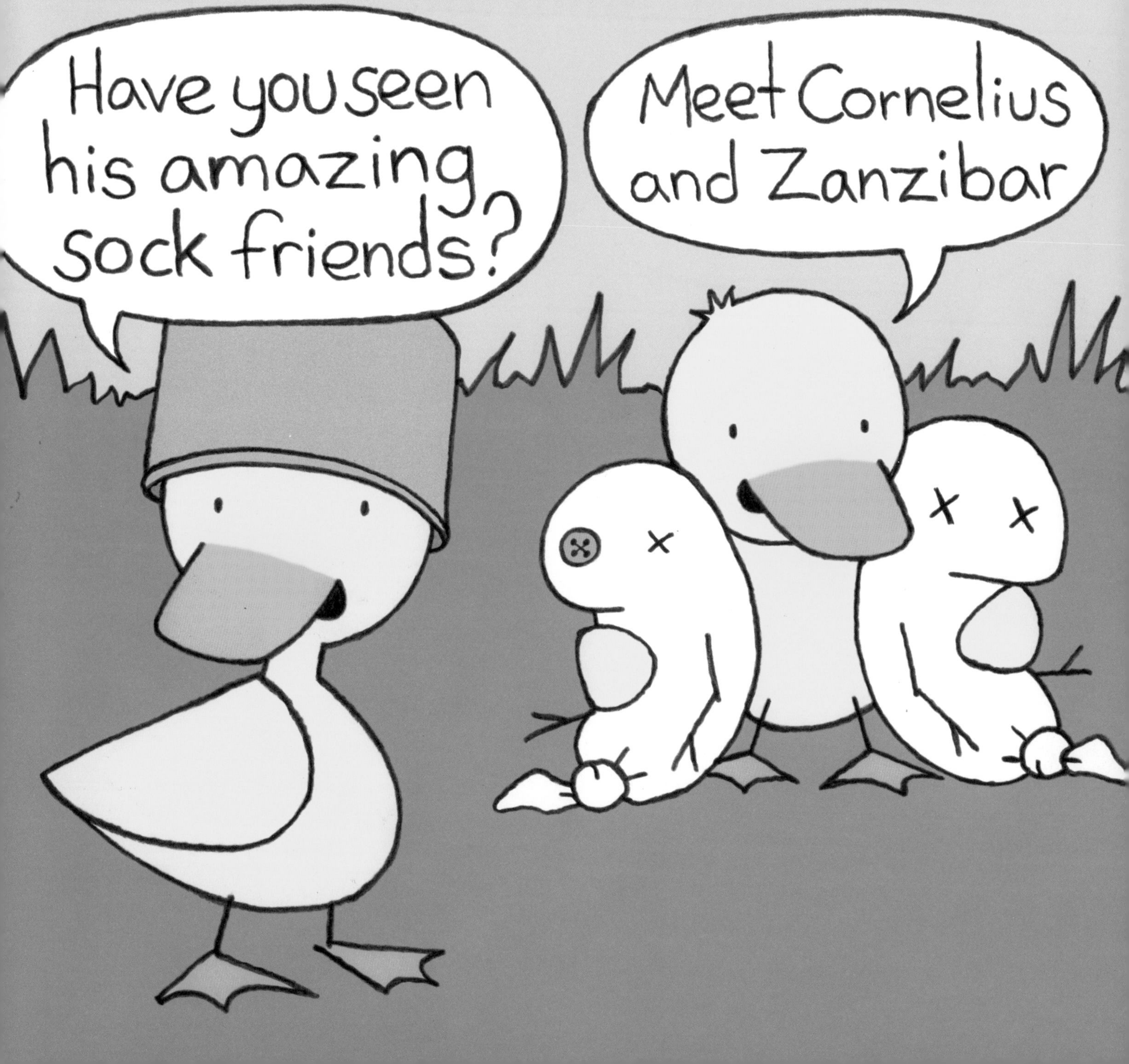
Have you seen his amazing sock friends?
Meet Cornelius and Zanzibar

Why do seagulls call them two dumb ducks?

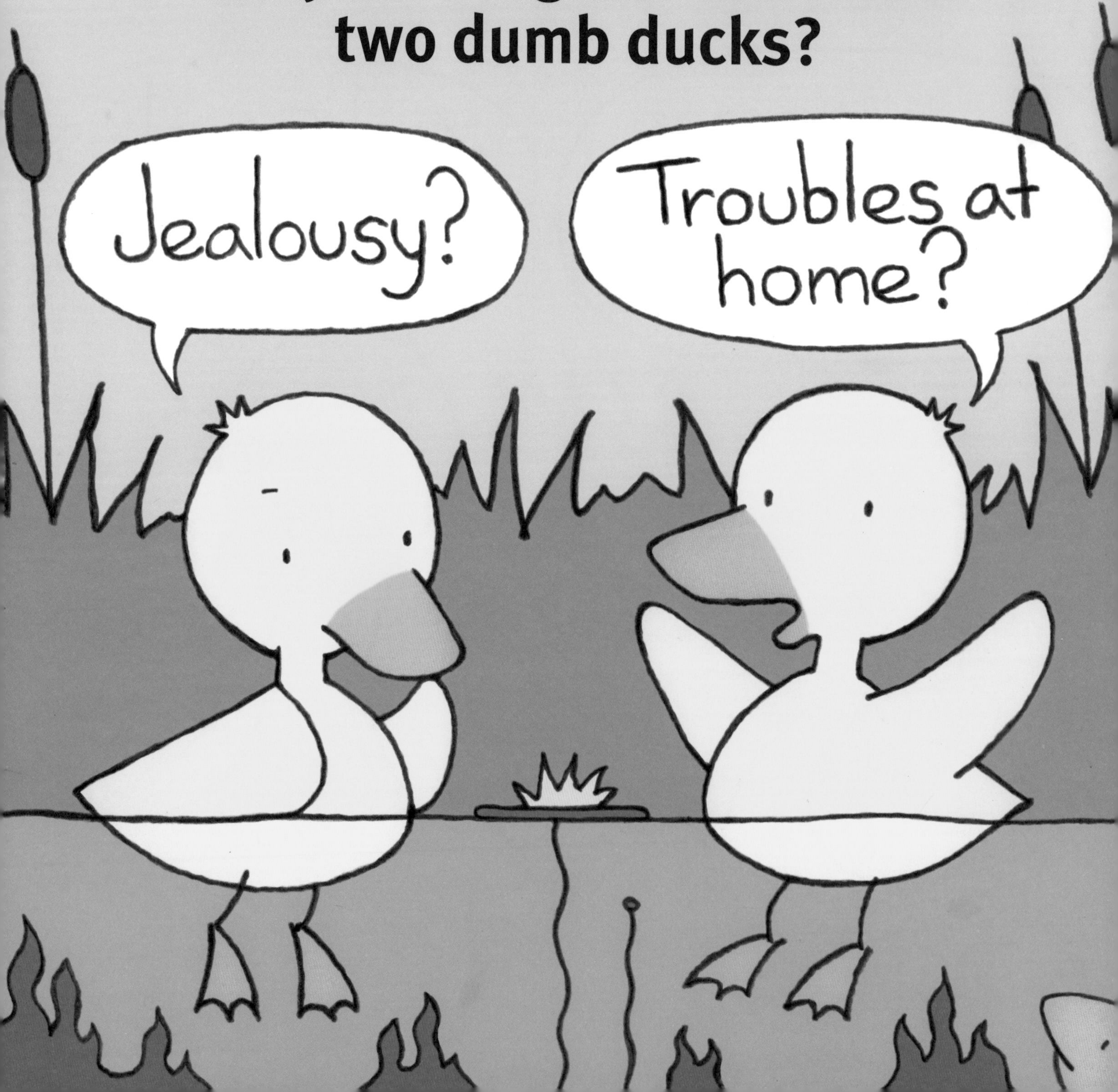
Jealousy?
Troubles at home?

Steve and Carl try asking the seagulls.

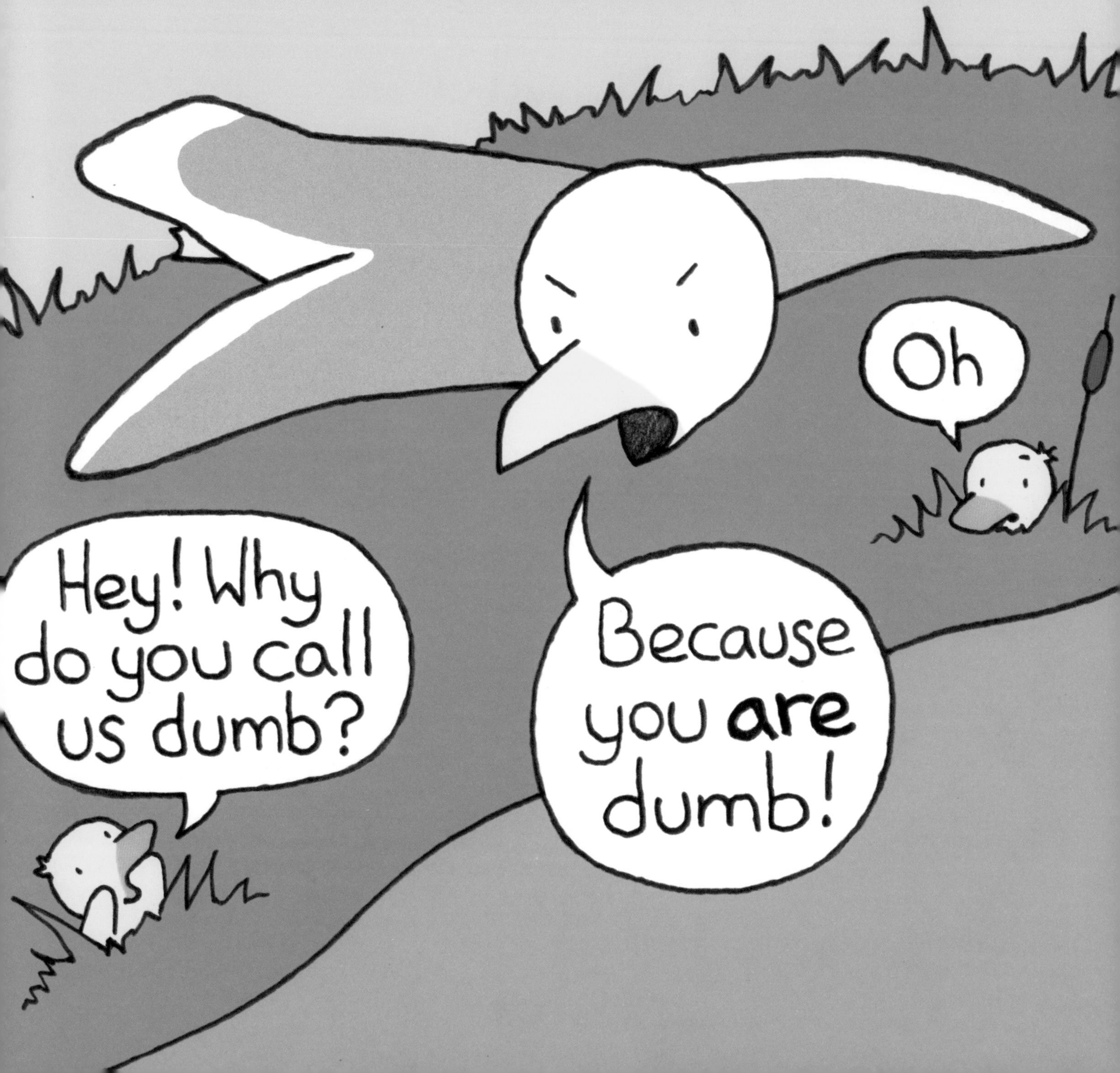
Hey! Why do you call us dumb?
Because you **are** dumb!
Oh

They try telling the seagulls to stop.

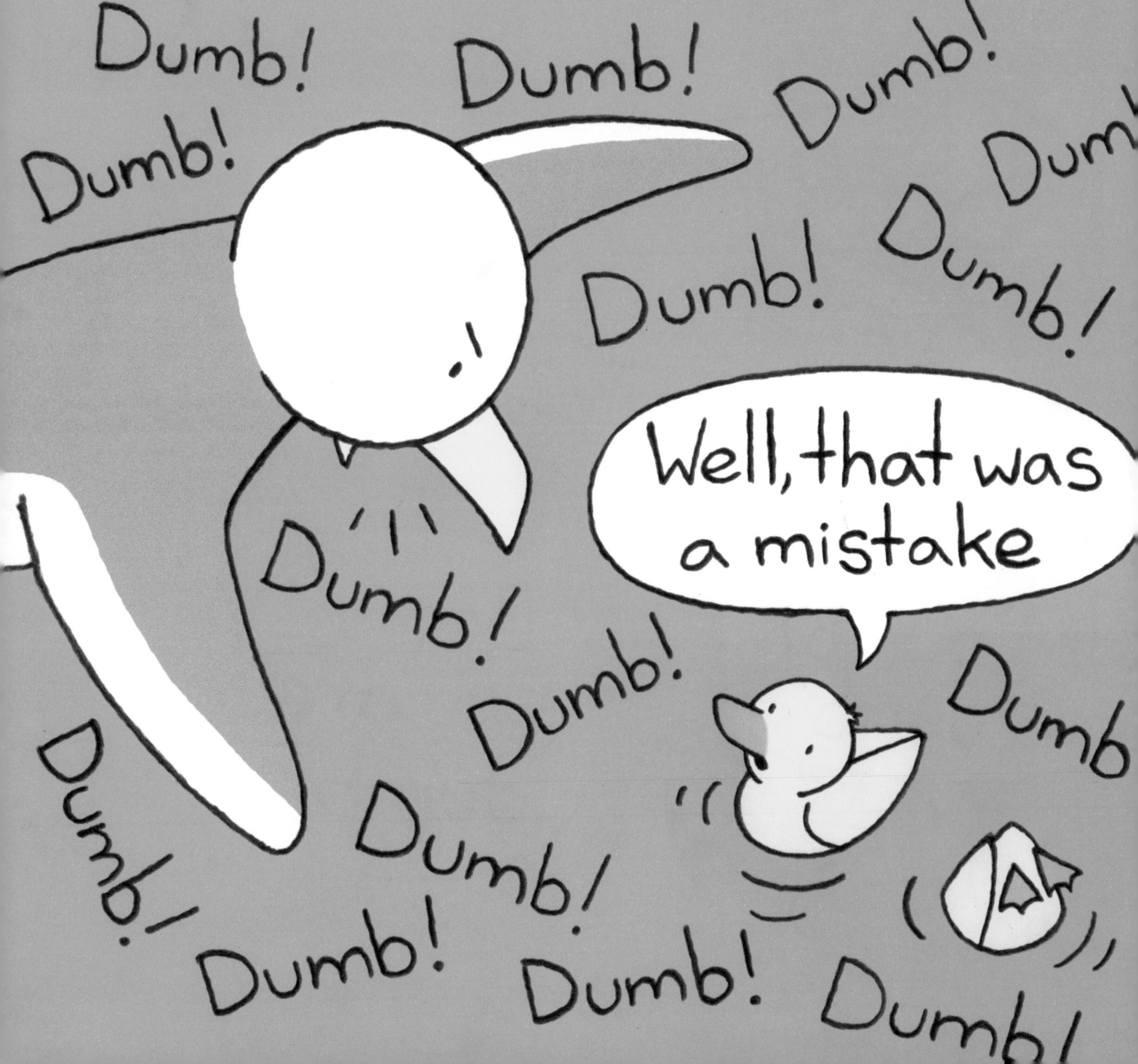
Dumb!
Dumb!
Dumb!
Dumb!
Dumb!
Dumb!
Well, that was a mistake
Dumb!
Dumb!
Dumb
Dumb!
Dumb!
Dumb!
Dumb!
Dumb!

They even try to look smarter.

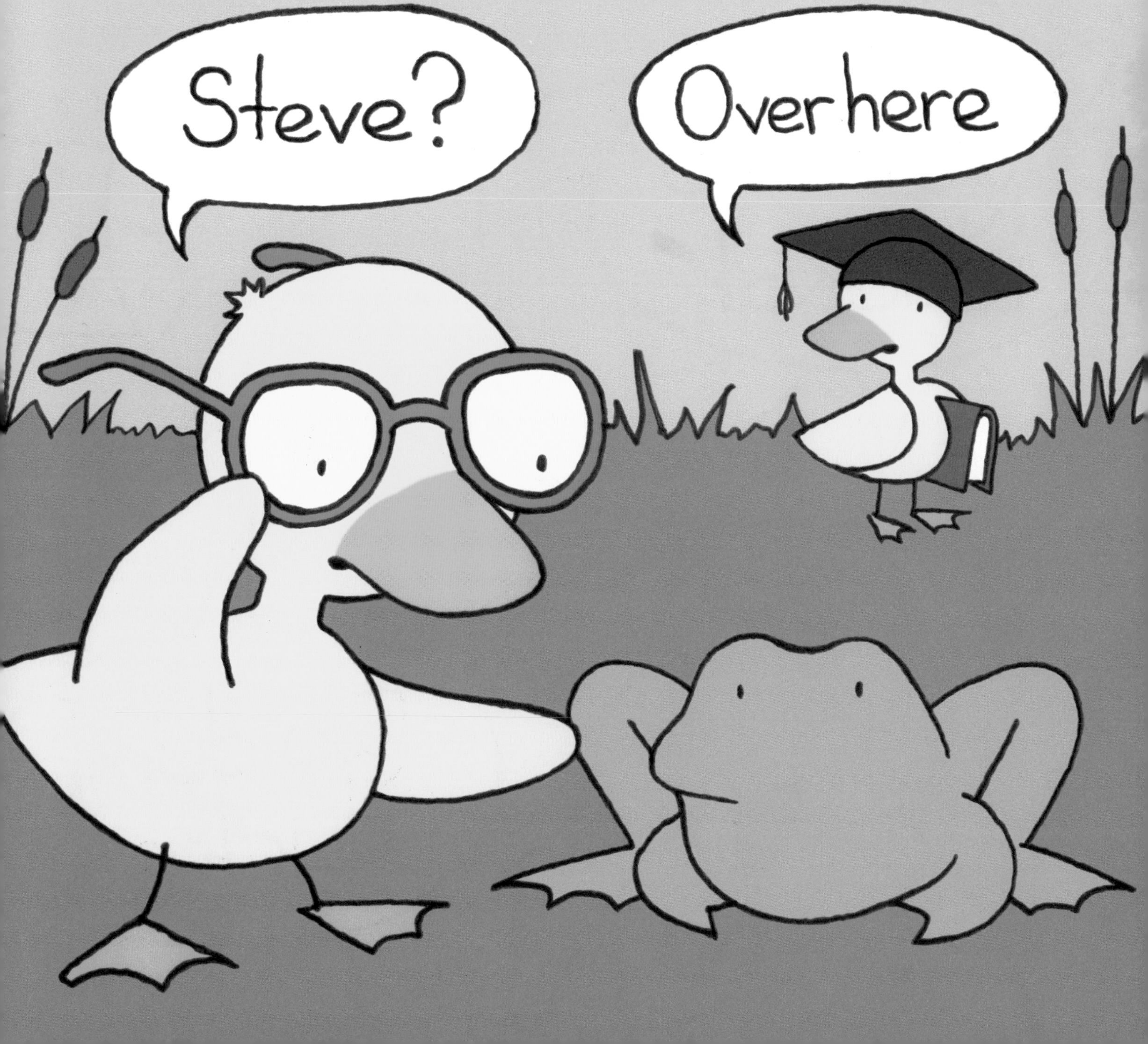
Steve?
Over here

But seagulls still call them . . .

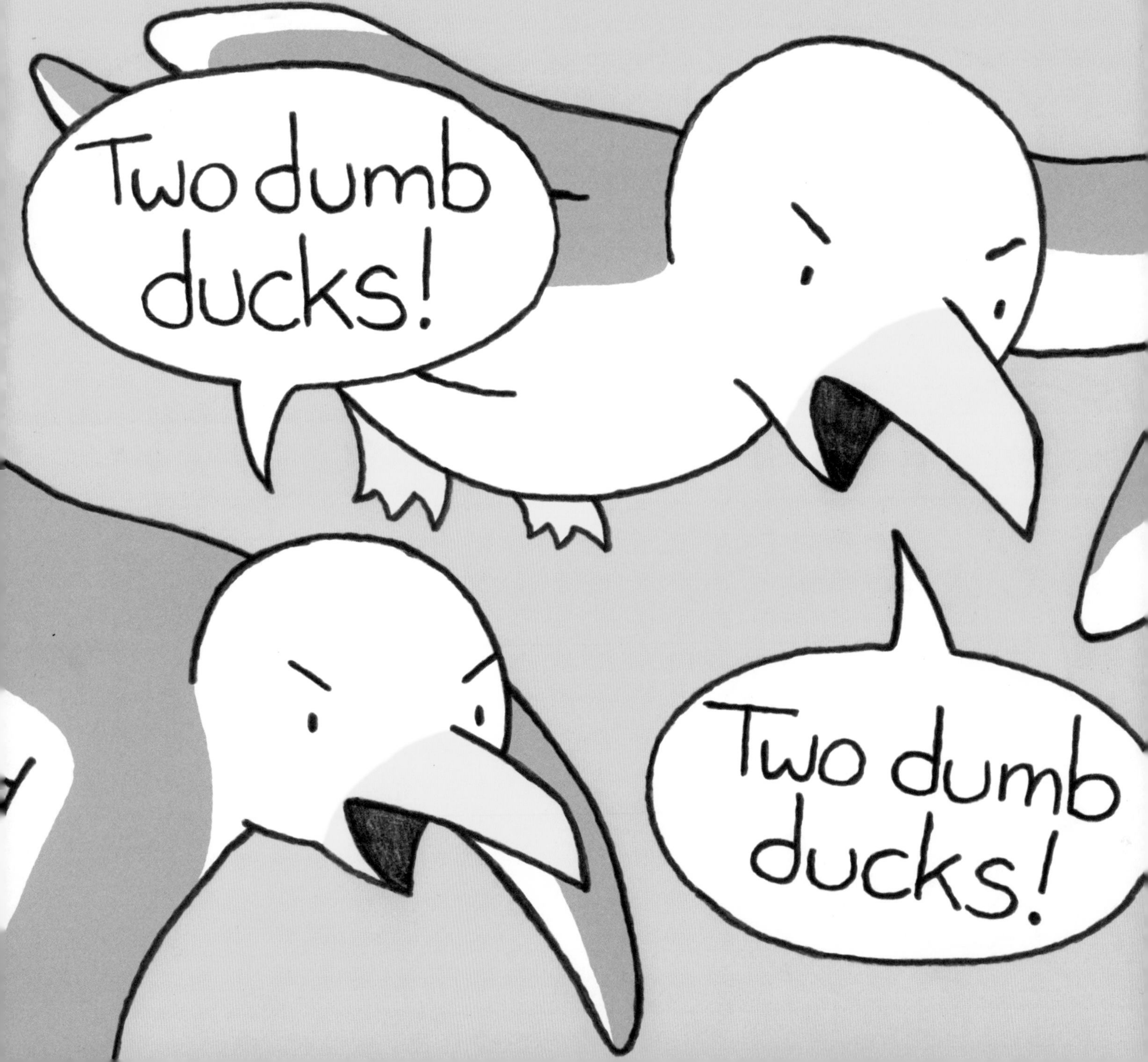
Two dumb ducks!
Two dumb ducks!

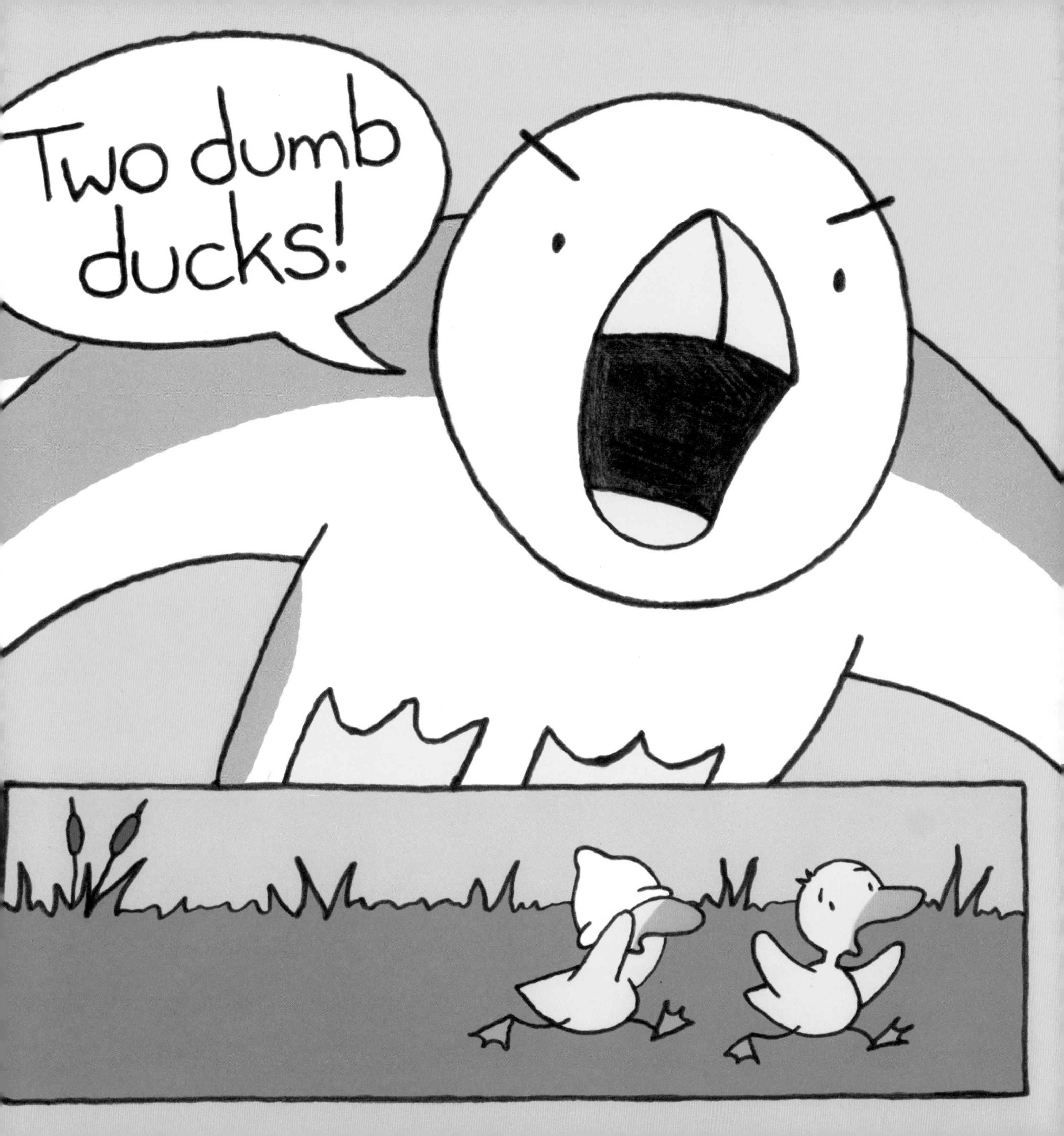
Two dumb ducks!

Steve and Carl get **MAD!**

Steve and Carl get **ANGRY!**

Steve and Carl get **EVEN....**

That night they sneak across the pond to search for the sleeping seagulls.

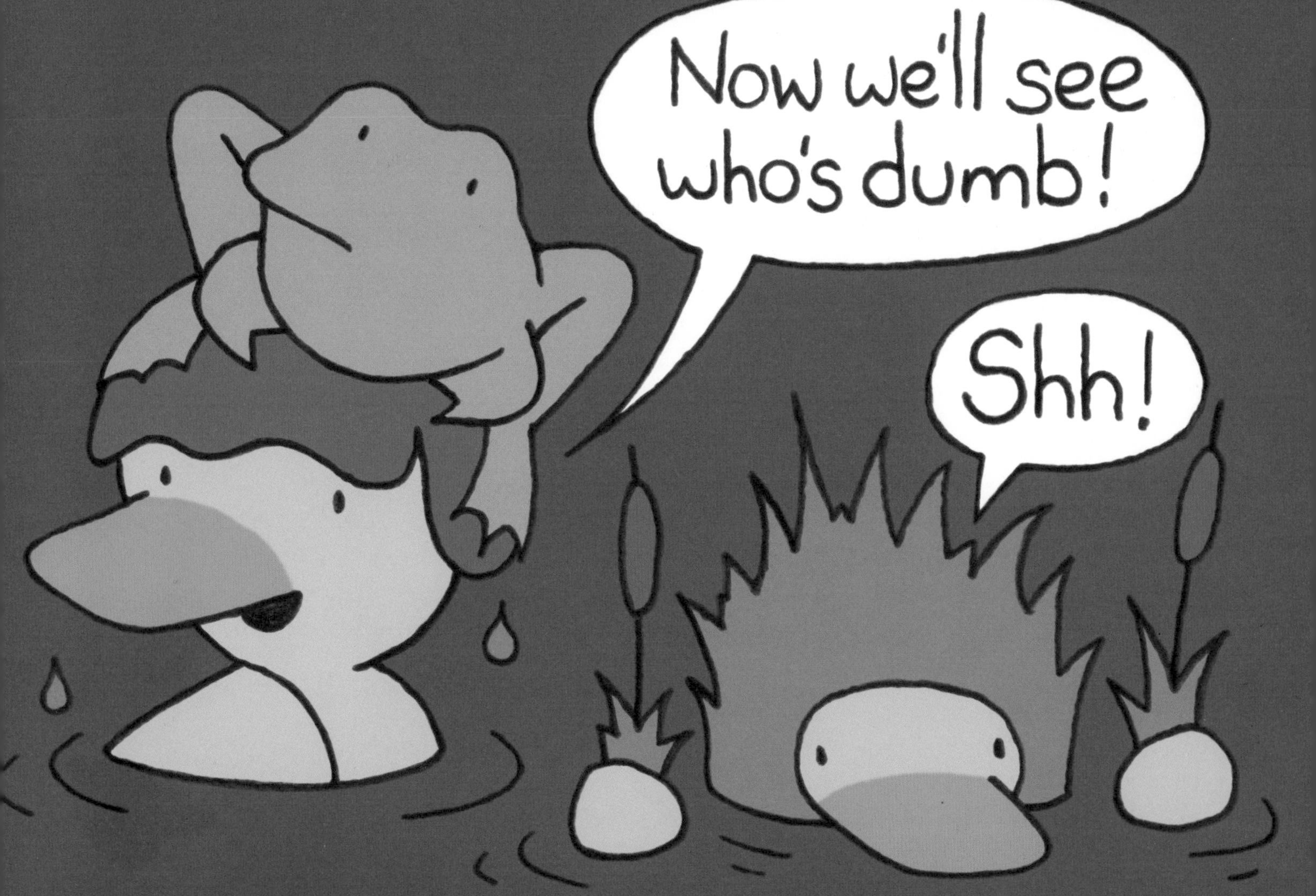
Now we'll see who's dumb!
Shh!

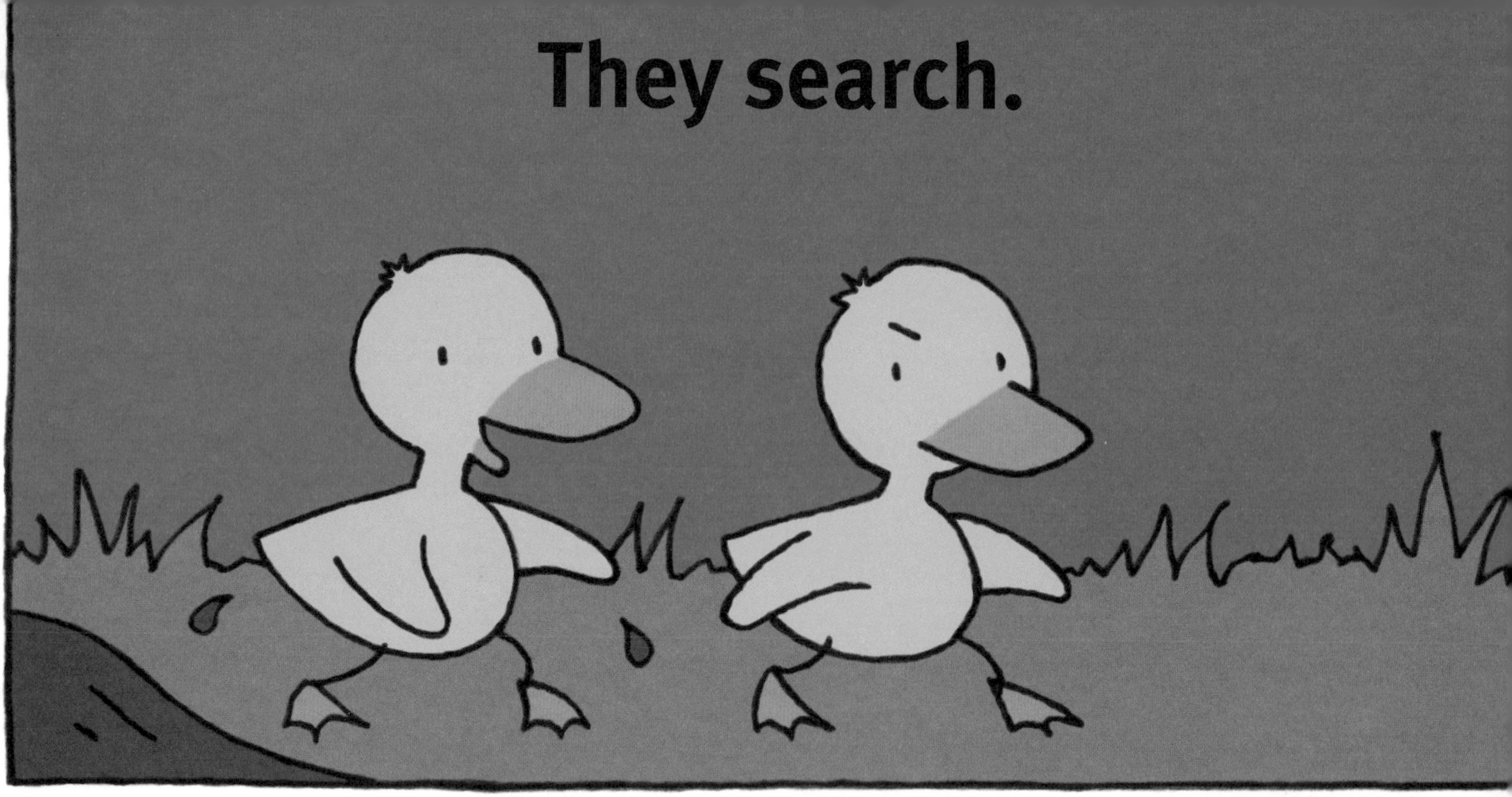
They search.

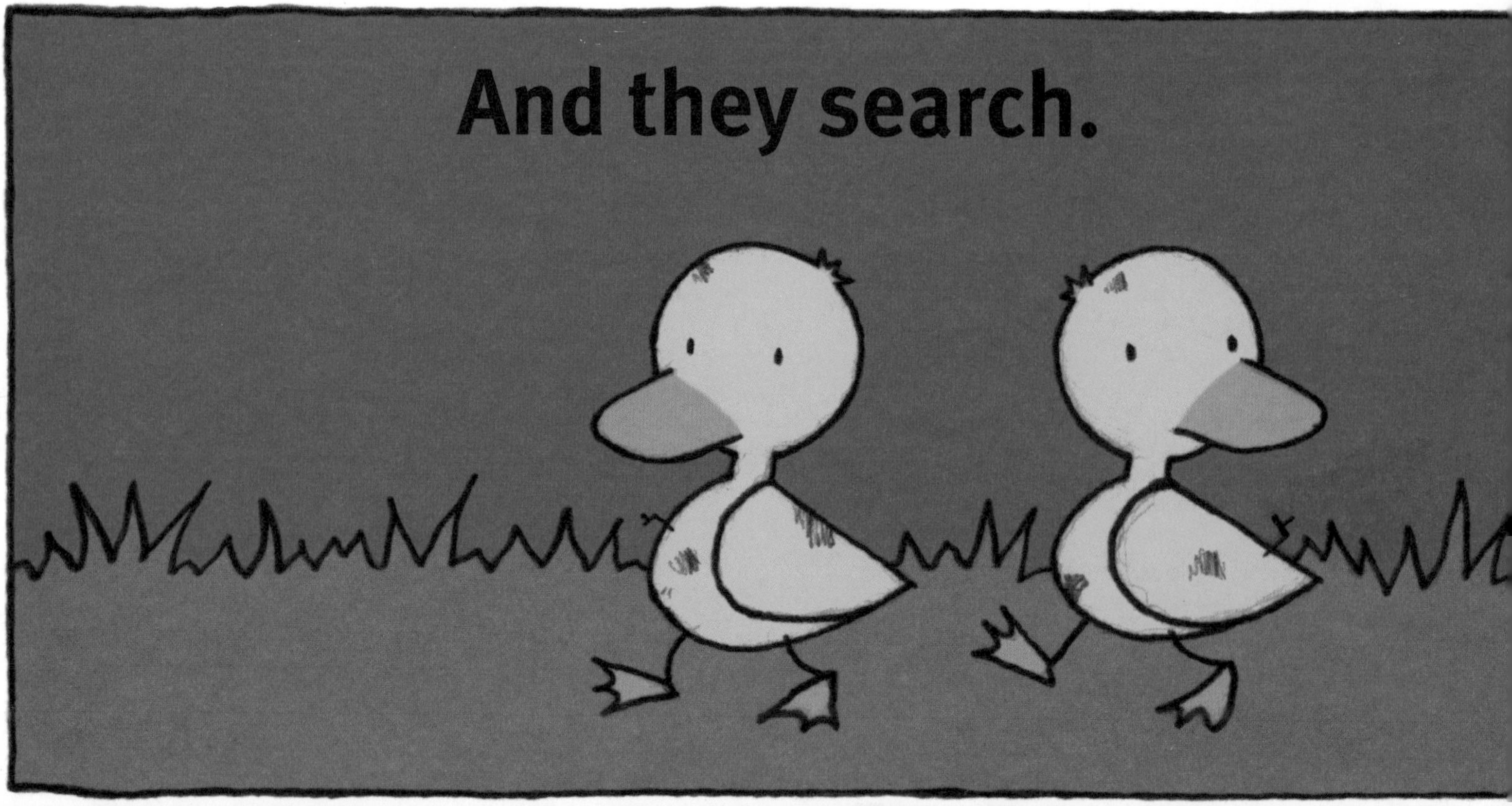
And they search.

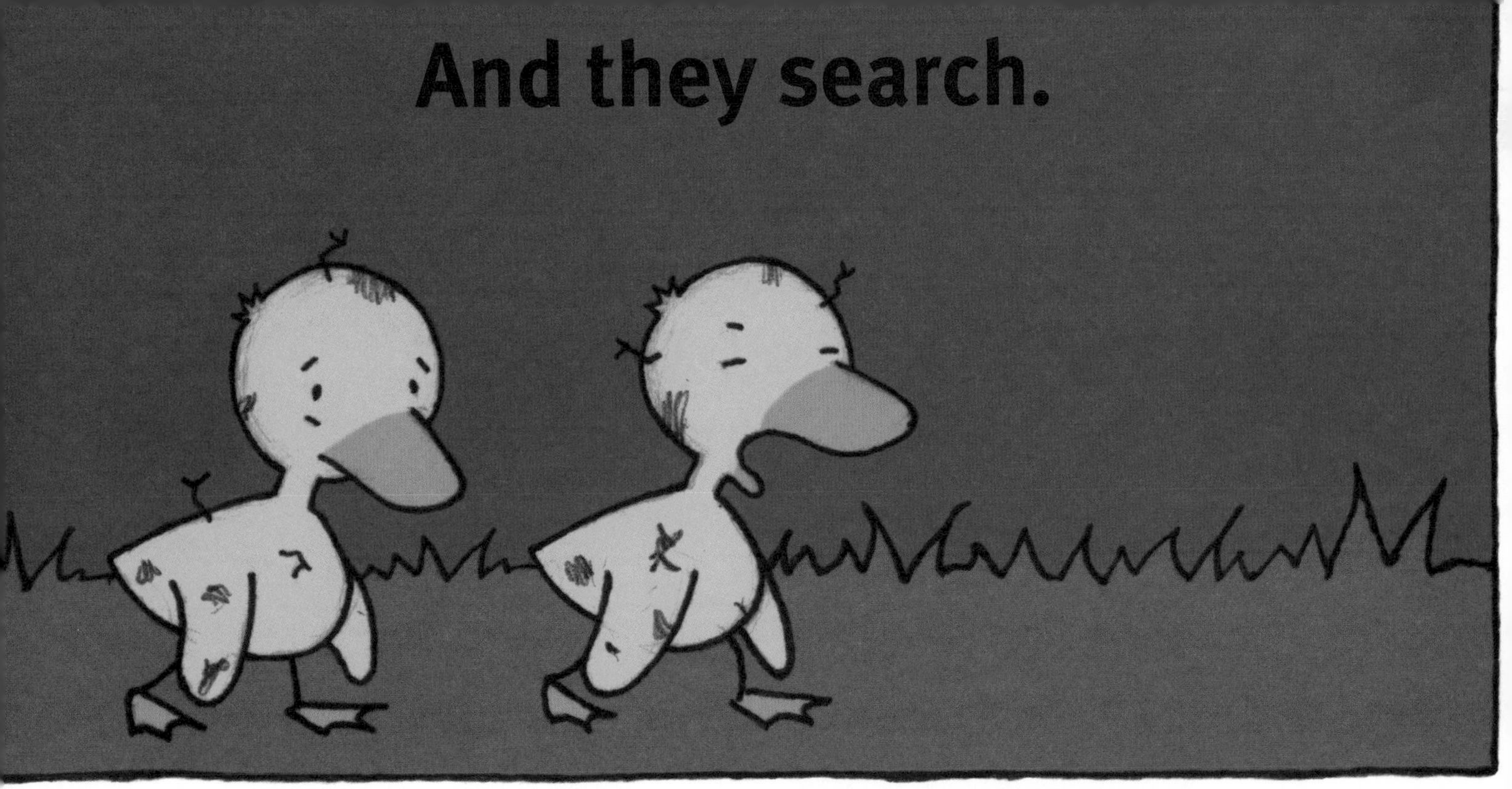
And they search.

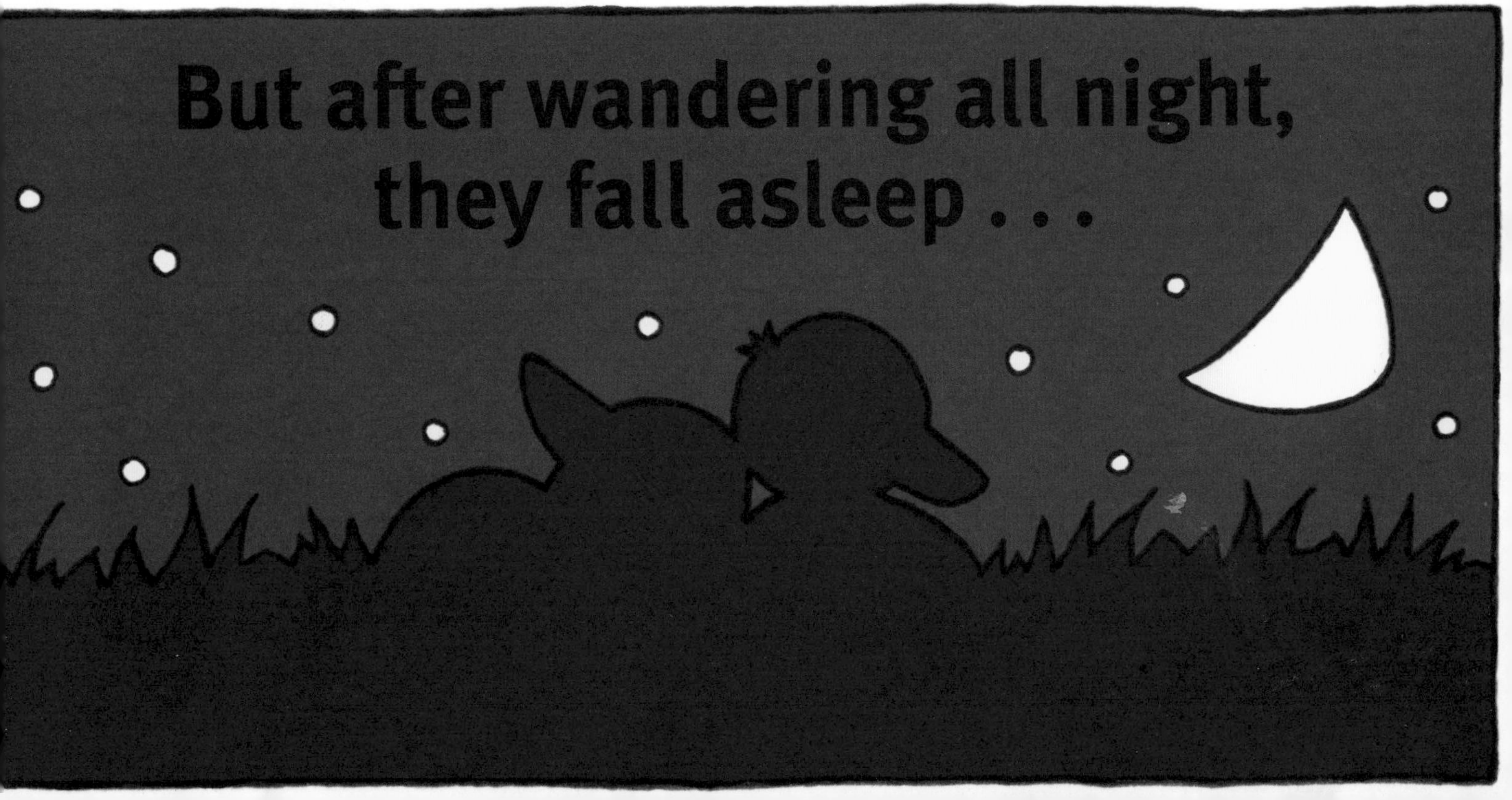
But after wandering all night,
they fall asleep . . .

and wake up in a puddle of muck!

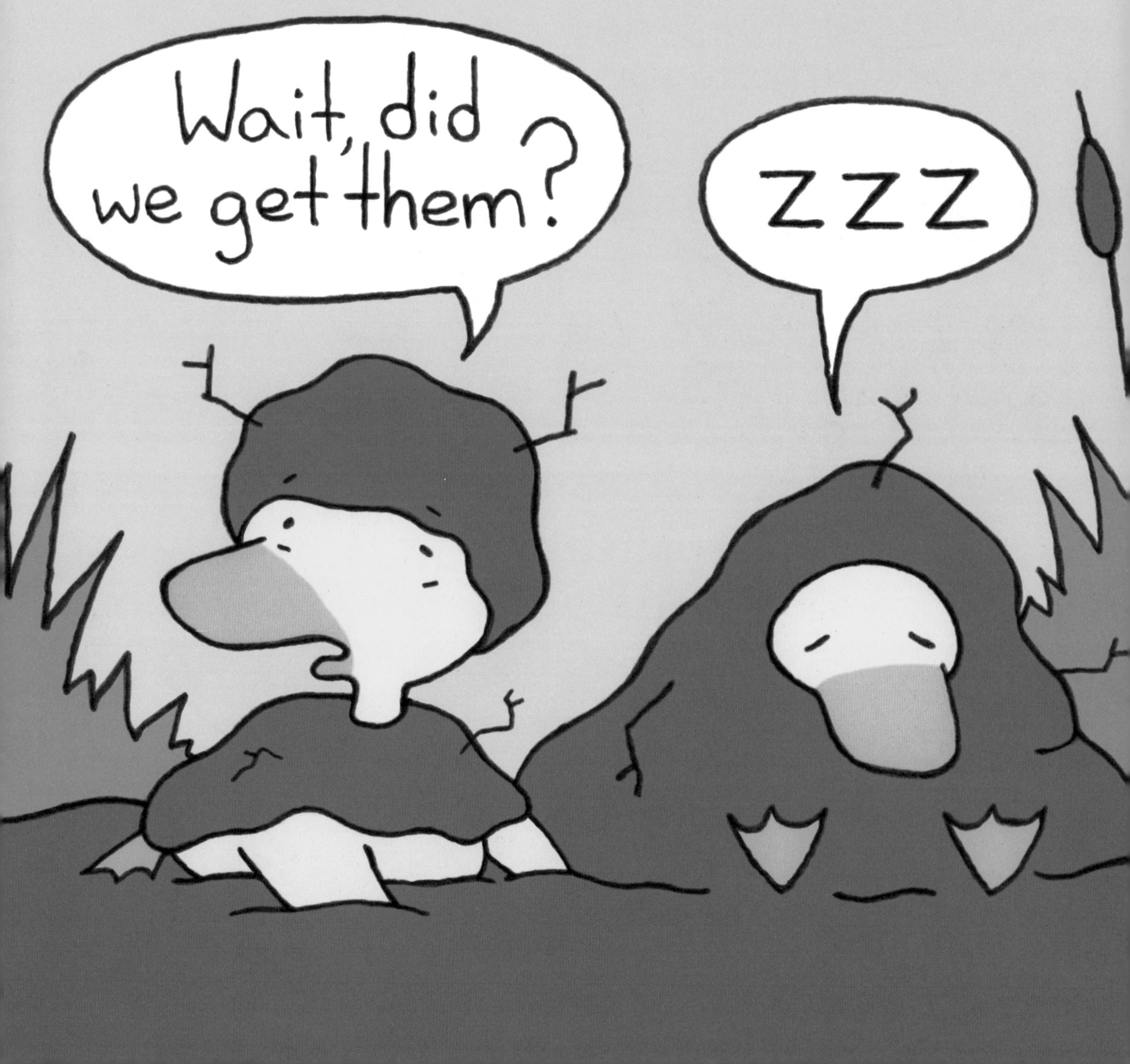
Wait, did we get them?
ZZZ

Yet Steve and Carl are not mad.

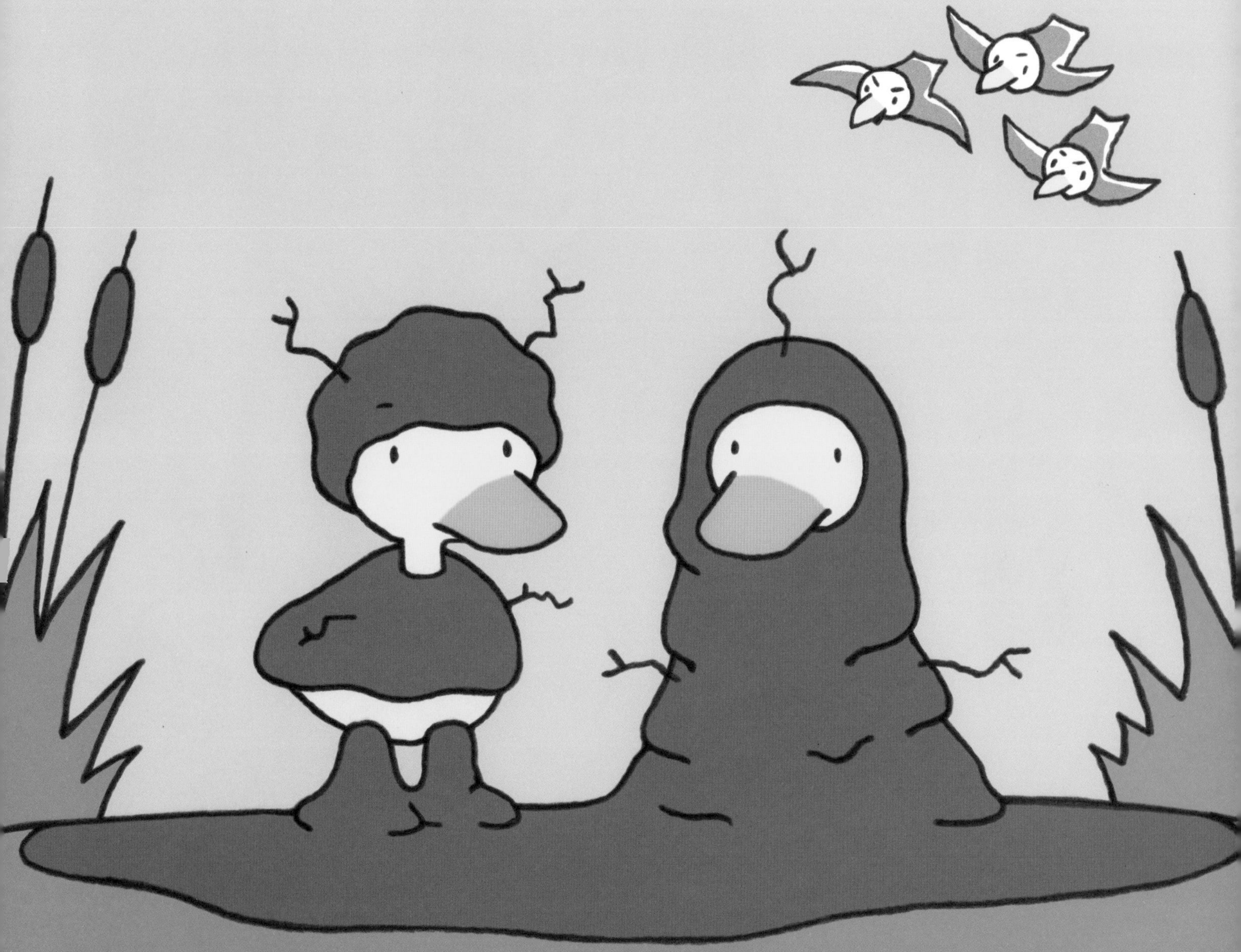

Steve and Carl are not angry.

Steve and Carl are FURIOUS!

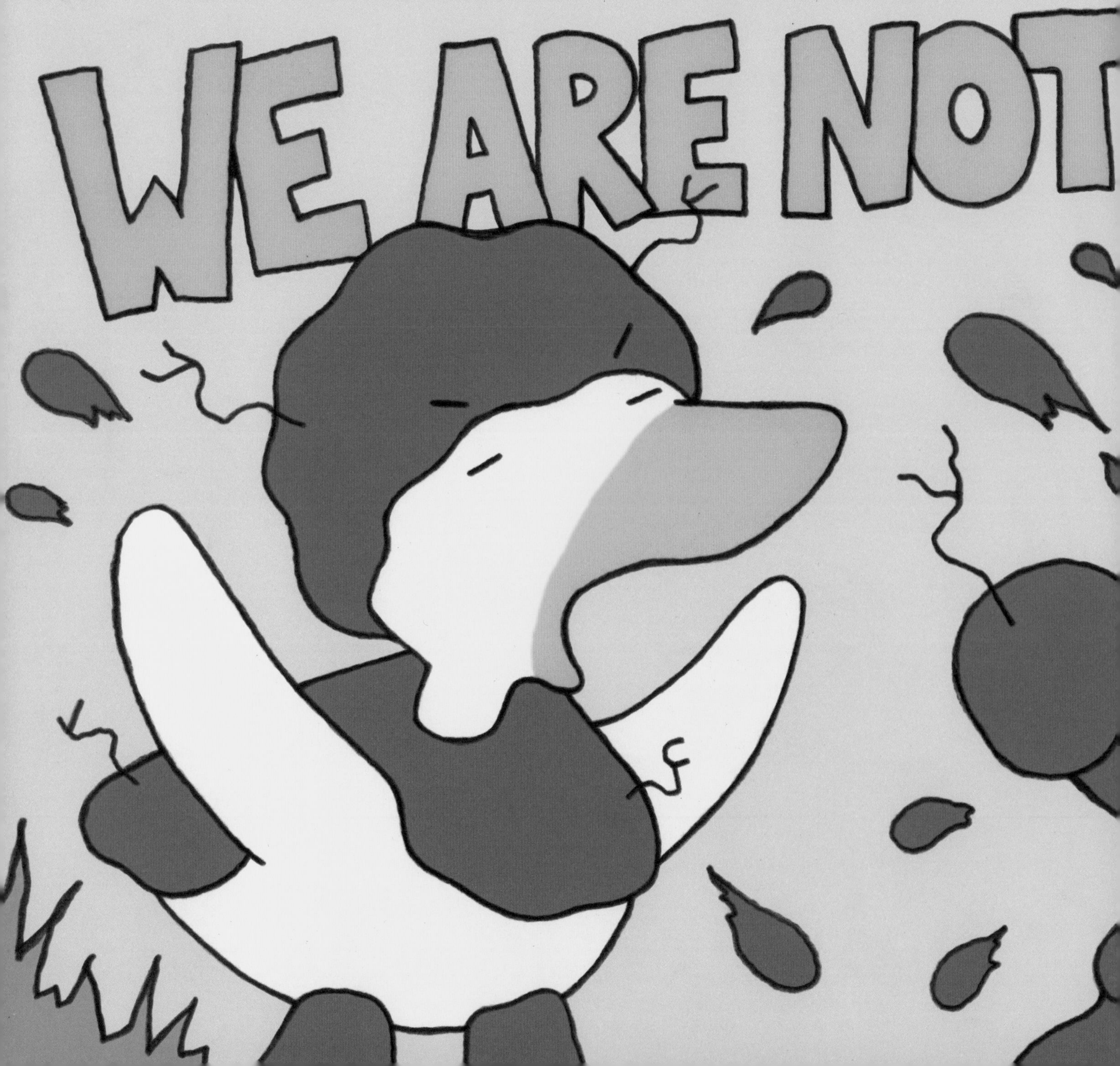
WE ARE NOT

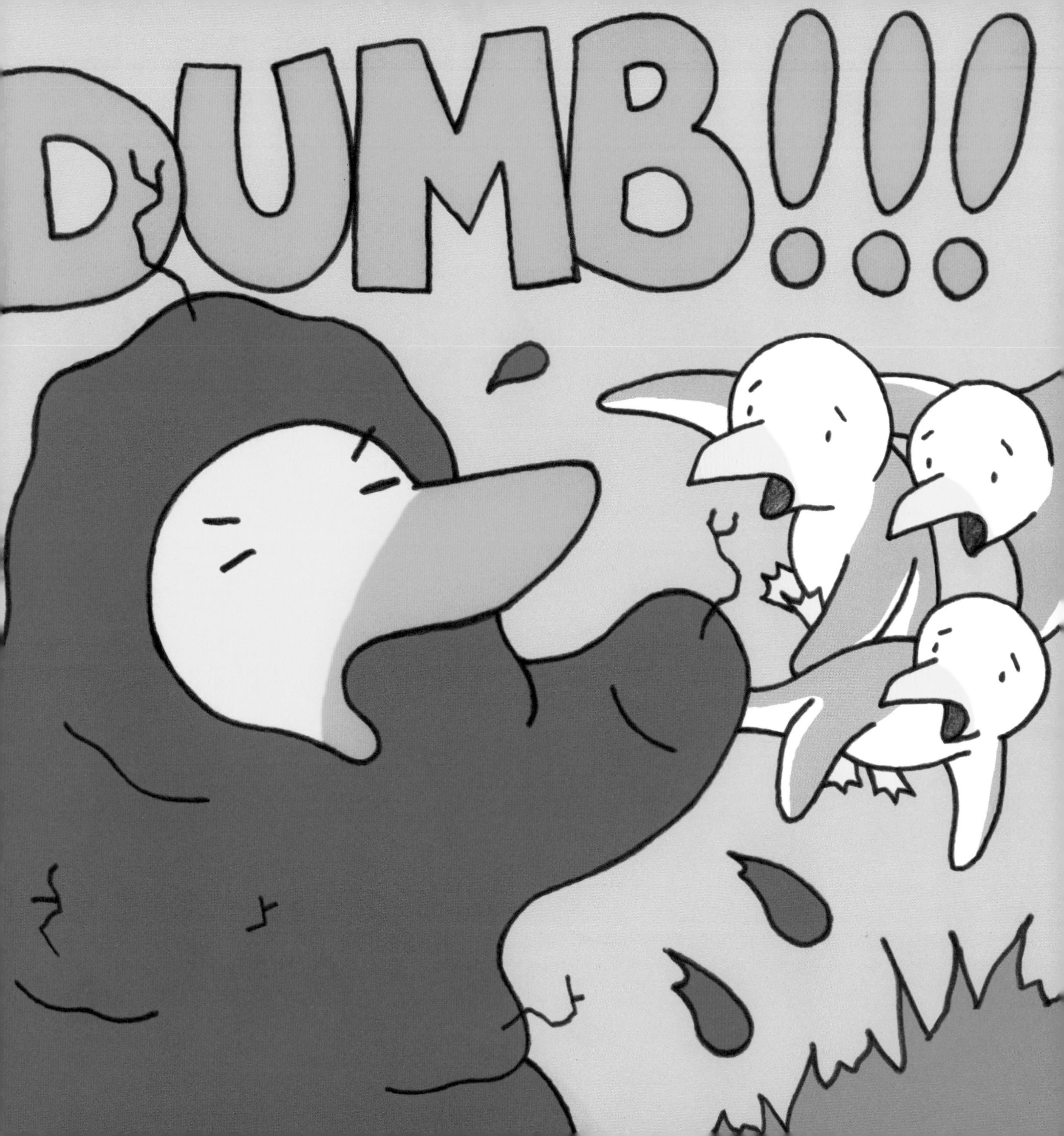
DUMB!!!

The seagulls dive behind a rock.

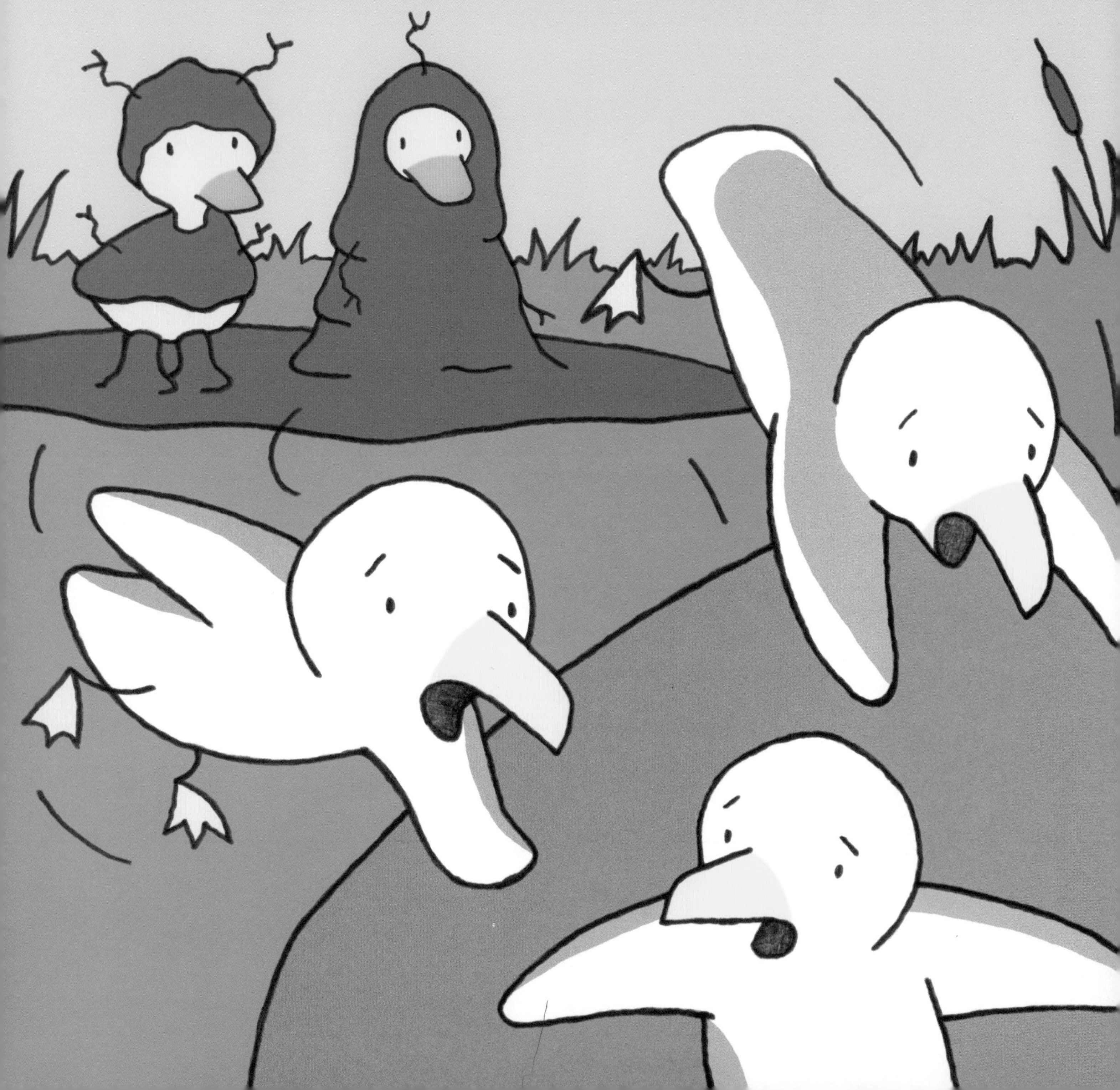

What are they afraid of?

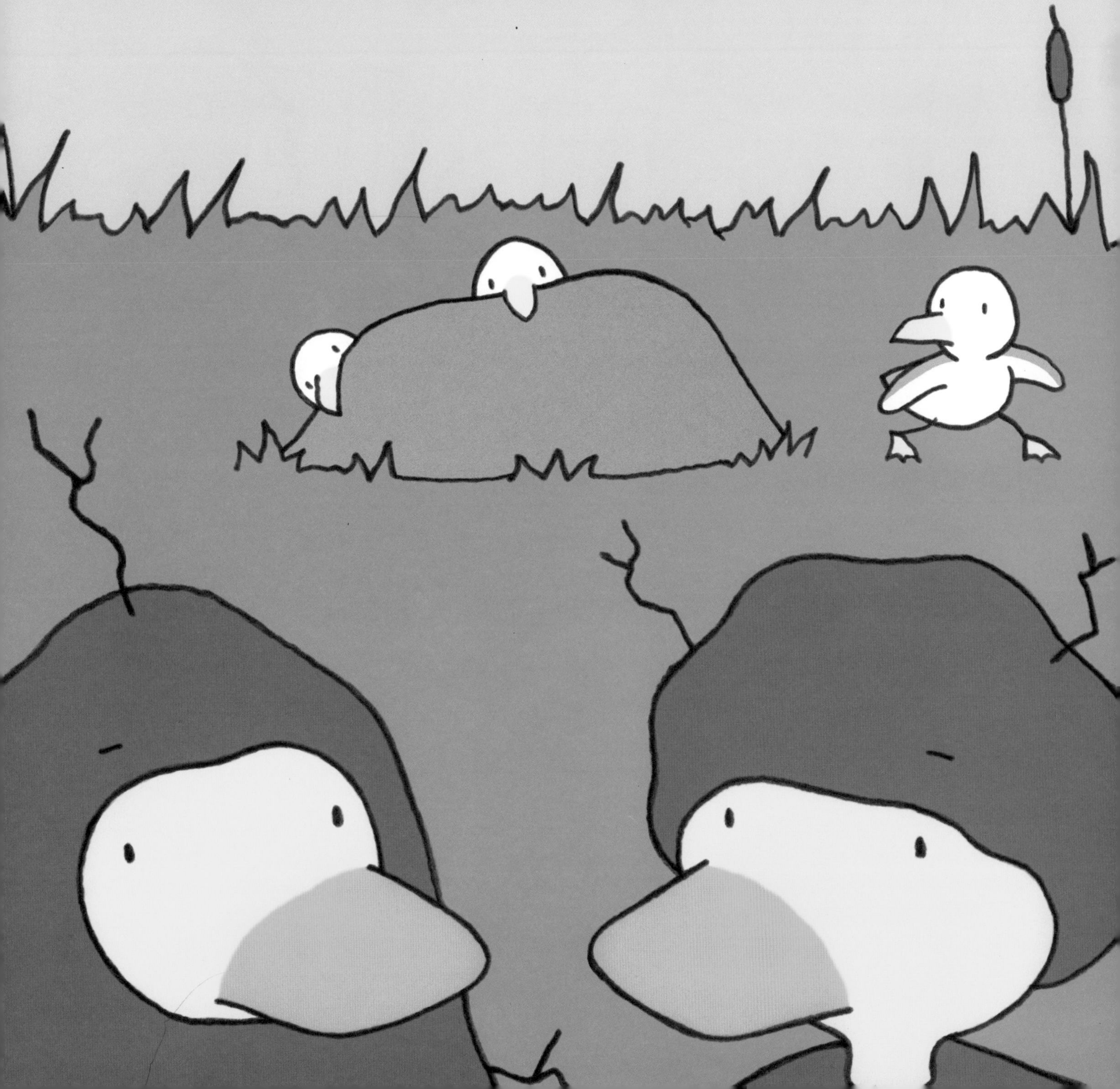

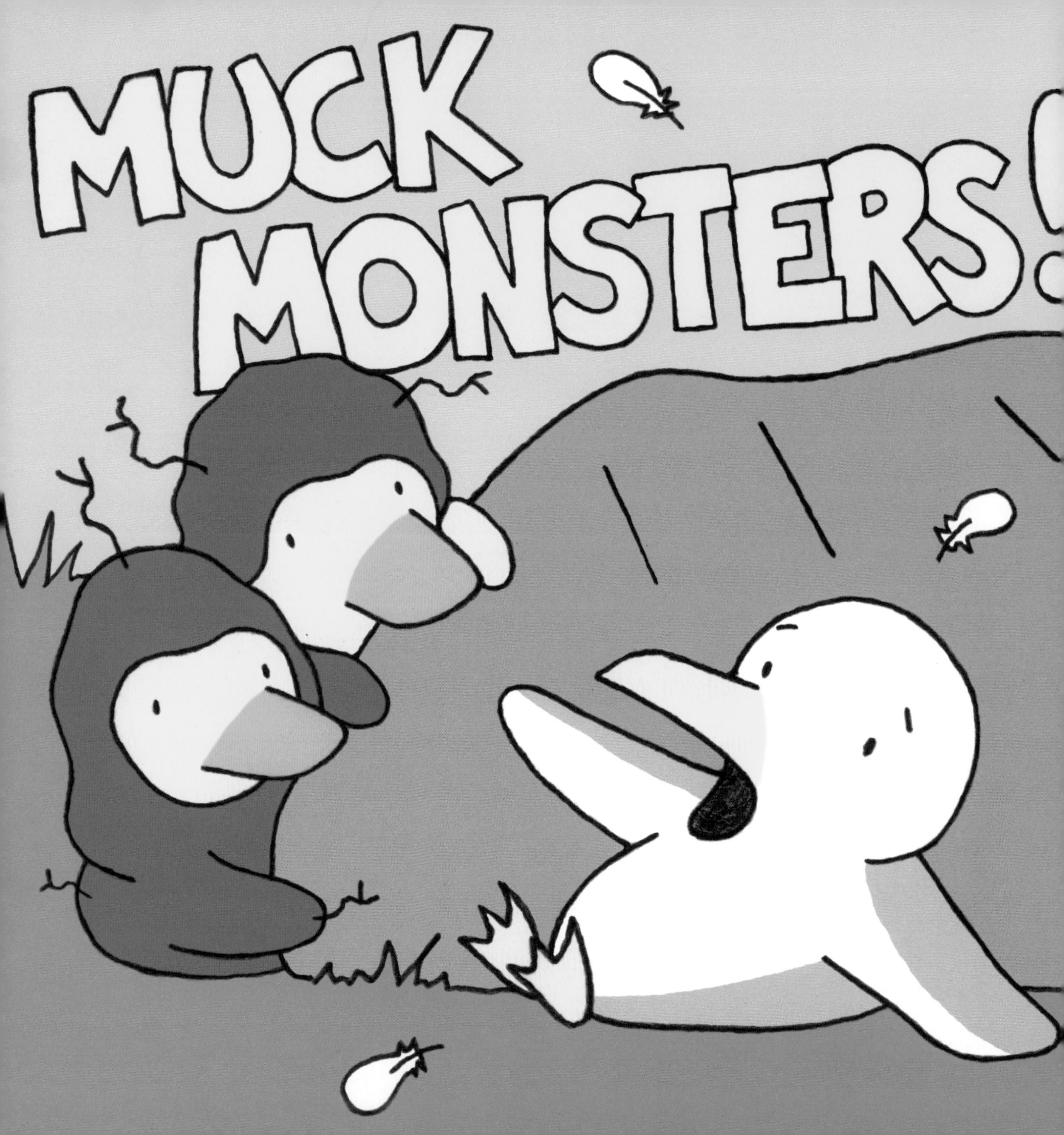
MUCK MONSTERS!

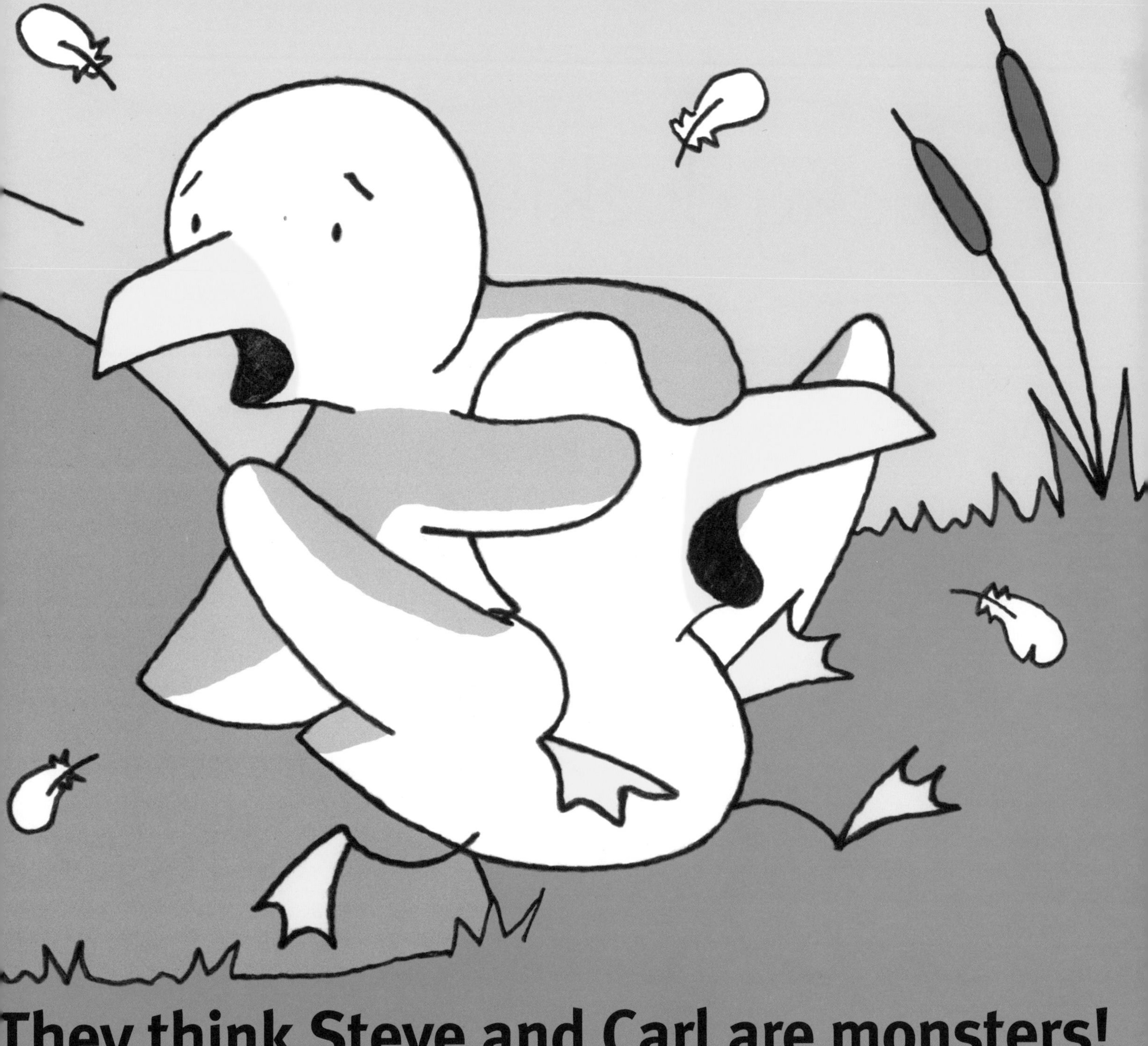

They think Steve and Carl are monsters!

But Steve and Carl are ducks.

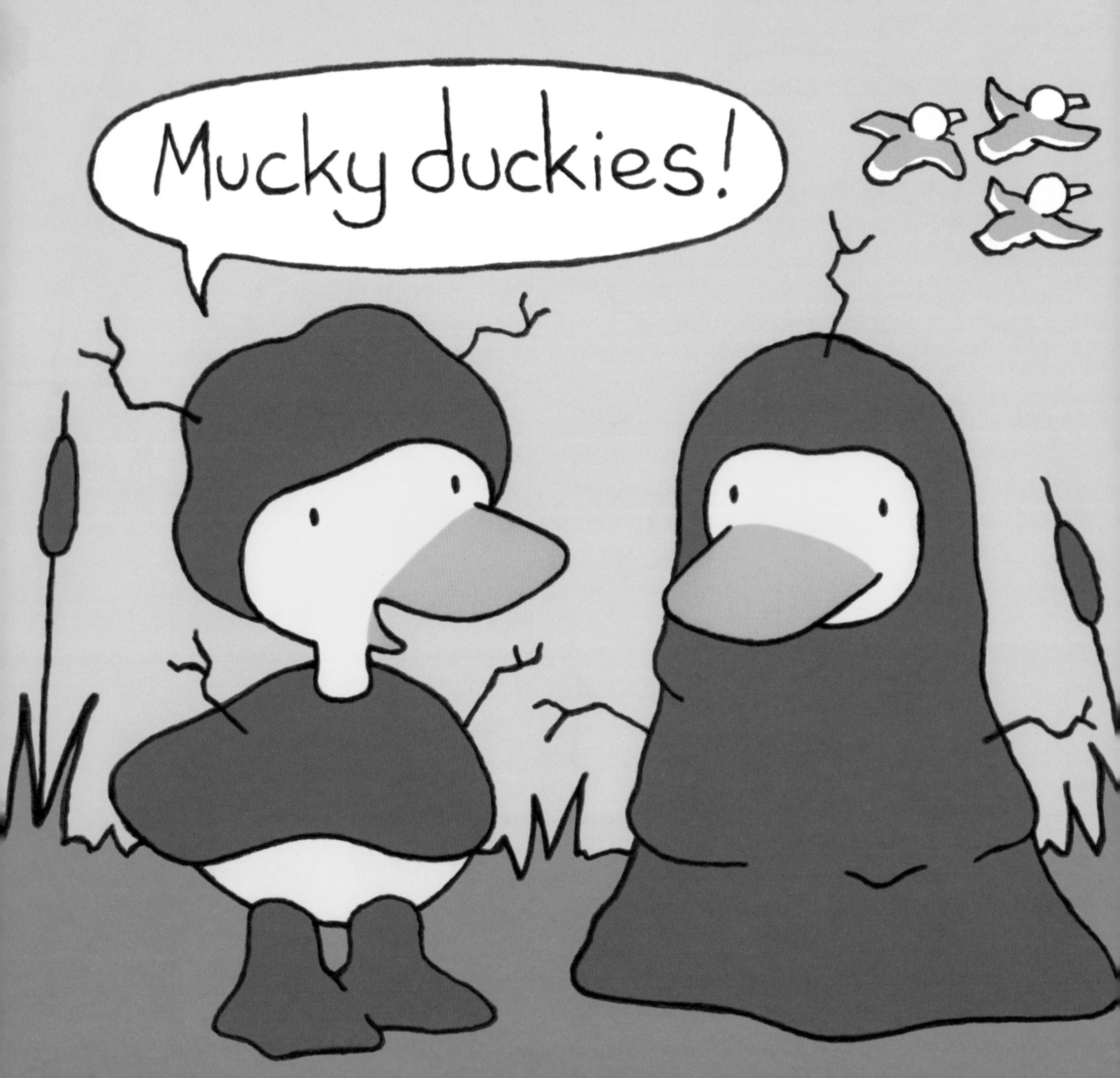
Mucky duckies!

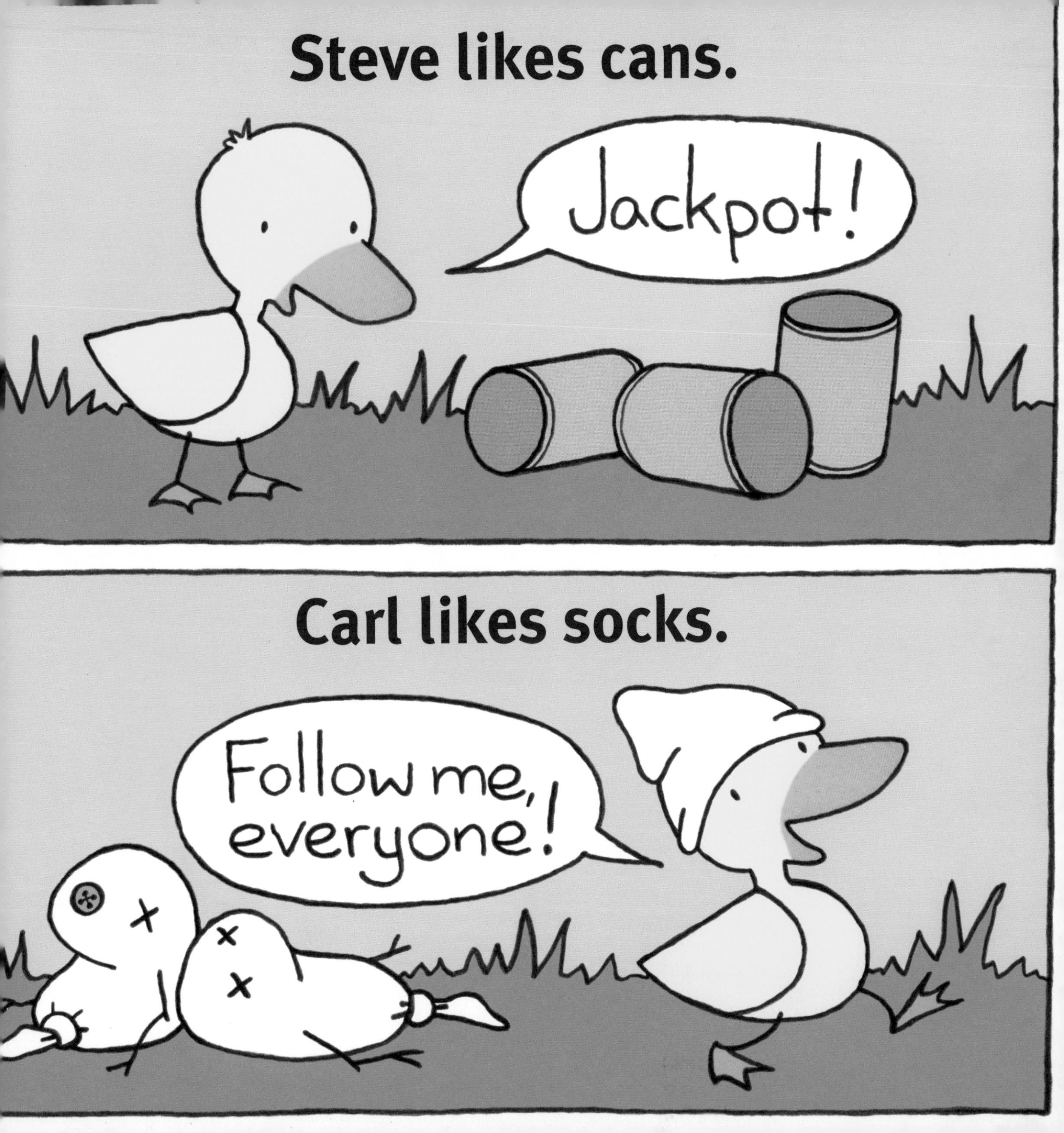
Steve likes cans.
Jackpot!
Carl likes socks.
Follow me, everyone!

Sometimes they like to play
Muck Monsters.

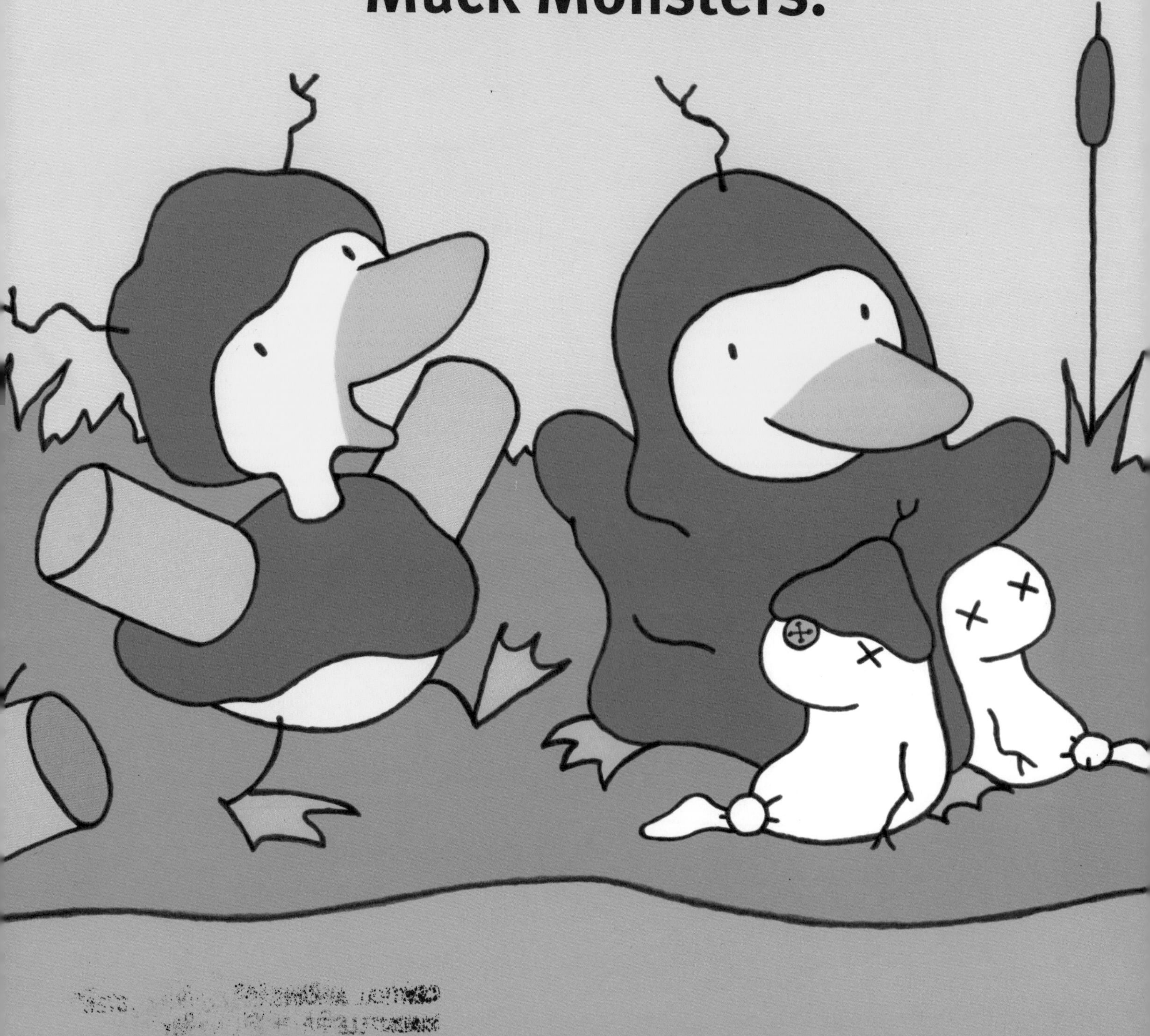

For Spiff

THIS IS A BORZOI BOOK PUBLISHED BY ALFRED A. KNOPF

Copyright © 2010 by Maxwell Eaton III

All rights reserved. Published in the United States by Alfred A. Knopf,

an imprint of Random House Children's Books,

a division of Random House, Inc., New York.

Knopf, Borzoi Books, and the colophon are registered

trademarks of Random House, Inc.

Visit us on the Web! www.randomhouse.com/kids

Educators and librarians, for a variety of teaching tools,

visit us at www.randomhouse.com/teachers

Library of Congress Cataloging-in-Publication Data

Eaton, Maxwell.

Two dumb ducks / by Maxwell Eaton III.

p. cm.

Summary: Steve and Carl, two ducks, decide to get even when the seagulls call them "dumb."

ISBN 978-0-375-84576-5 (trade) — ISBN 978-0-375-94576-2 (lib. bdg.)

[1. Teasing—Fiction. 2. Ducks—Fiction. 3. Seagulls—Fiction.] I. Title.

PZ7.E3892Tw 2010   [E]—dc22   2010004959

The illustrations in this book were created using graphite pencil with digital coloring.

MANUFACTURED IN CHINA

October 2010   10 9 8 7 6 5 4 3 2 1

First Edition